The Play

by Caroline Majors

illustrated by Julie Durrell

 HOUGHTON MIFFLIN   BOSTON

On Saturday, Marilyn went with her parents to see *Alice in Wonderland* at the Community Theater. Marilyn had never seen anything so wonderful. Right there she made up her mind to be an actress.

Mr. Randall, the theater director, was a friend
of Marilyn's father. After the show, Mr. Randall
invited Marilyn and her family to go backstage.
There Marilyn met Ms. Highland, who had
played the Queen of Hearts.

Meeting a real actress thrilled Marilyn. "I want to be an actress too," Marilyn said.

"Maybe you will be," replied Ms. Highland with a smile.

On Sunday night, just after dinner, the phone rang. Marilyn's mother talked for a few minutes. Then she handed the phone to Marilyn.

"It's Mr. Randall, the theater director," Mom said. "He wants to talk to you."

"Do you still want to be an actress?" Mr. Randall asked.

Marilyn said she did.

"Then come to the theater Saturday at one o'clock," said Mr. Randall. "We're having tryouts for our new play."

6

On Saturday, Mr. Randall asked Marilyn to read a few lines from the new play. It was called *Signs of Spring*.

When Marilyn finished reading, the director smiled. "That was perfect," he said. "You'll be great playing the part of the daughter."

Every day after school, Marilyn did her
homework. Then she practiced her lines. By the
end of the week, she had memorized them all.

When Marilyn arrived for rehearsal the next Saturday, she was a little nervous. Finally, it was her turn to speak. Ms. Highland had just finished speaking her lines to one of the other actors. She was playing the lead role in the play.

Marilyn knew her lines. She had said them to her father at the breakfast table. She had said them to her mother in the car. She had even said them to Mr. Randall in the theater lobby.

But when she stood up on stage, the words wouldn't come out. She was just too scared.

Marilyn talked about the problem with her parents.

"Just try to relax," Mother said.

But Marilyn could not relax.

"There's no reason to be afraid," Father said.

But Marilyn **was** afraid.

At the next rehearsal, Ms. Highland put her arm around Marilyn. "I get nervous on stage too," she admitted. Then she told Marilyn about a special way she had to make herself feel better. When she said her lines, she pretended that only her husband was in the room.

"Try it," Ms. Highland said. "When you say your lines, pretend you are talking only to me."

When it was Marilyn's turn to speak, she tried to think only of Ms. Highland. It worked pretty well, but she still forgot a few lines.

"Don't worry," Ms. Highland said afterwards. "You'll get better with time."

At the dress rehearsal, everyone wore their costumes. With the stage lights in her eyes, Marilyn couldn't see Ms. Highland. But she said her lines to Ms. Highland anyway. She was delighted when she forgot only one line.

On the night of the opening performance, the theater was packed. Marilyn peeked through the curtains nervously as the musicians picked up their instruments. Suddenly, she felt a hand on her shoulder. It was Ms. Highland.

"Remember," Ms. Highland said with a wink, "say your lines only to me."

Finally, it was time for Marilyn's lines. As she walked out onto the stage, her heart beat madly. The theater was packed with people, but Marilyn thought about only one of them.

That night, her performance was perfect.